JJ Gorbachev, V

JJ Gorbachev, V

Valeri Gorbachev
Nicky and the Rainy Day

A CHESHIRE STUDIO BOOK
North-South Books · New York · London

It was a rainy day. Nicky and his brothers and sisters couldn't go out to play.

"It's awful to be stuck inside all day," said Nicky. "It's so boring."

Everyone agreed.

"Mother," said Nathan, "we're bored."

"We don't like the rain," said Nora.

"Yes," said Nellie. "We can't go outside."

"There's nothing to do," said Ned.

"Why don't you read a book or play cards while I fix lunch?" said Mother Rabbit.

"I have a better idea," said Nicky. "We can go to the desert."

"The desert is sunny and bright, with beautiful yellow sand, and it never rains there."

"No, no," said Mother Rabbit. "That's impossible."
"Why not?" asked Nathan. "It's a great idea!"

"But it's so hot in the desert," said Nora.
"Yes," said Nellie. "And there's nothing to drink there."
"And we could get lost," said Ned.
"Okay," said Nicky. "Then we'll go to the mountains."

"The mountains are very big, with beautiful blue cliffs."

"No, no," said Mother Rabbit. "That's impossible."
"Why not?" asked Nathan. "It's a great idea!"

"But there are landslides in the mountains," said Nora.
"Yes, and mountain lions, too!" said Nellie.
"And we could get lost," said Ned.
"Okay," said Nicky. "Then we'll go to the jungle."

"The jungle is leafy and green and very beautiful."

"No, no," said Mother Rabbit. "That's impossible."
"Why not?" asked Nathan. "It's a great idea!"

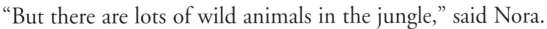

"But there are lots of wild animals in the jungle," said Nora.
"Yes, and snakes, too!" said Nellie.
"And we could get lost," said Ned.
"Okay," said Nicky. "Then we'll go to the South Pole."

"The South Pole has lots of beautiful white snow."

"No, no," said Mother Rabbit. "That's impossible."
"Why not?" asked Nathan. "It's a great idea!"

"But it's freezing cold at the South Pole," said Nora.
"Yes, and there are blizzards, too!" said Nellie.
"And we could get lost," said Ned.
"Okay," said Nicky. "Then we'll go to outer space."

"Outer space is filled with beautiful red and orange planets."

"No!" said Mother Rabbit. "We're not going to outer space. We are going for a walk in the meadow. Look! The rain has stopped and the sun is coming out."

"Hurray!" cried all the little rabbits.

They put on their raincoats and boots and headed outside.

"Isn't it nice to go for a walk after the rain?" asked Mother Rabbit.

"Oh, yes!" agreed Nicky and his brothers and sisters as they splashed in the puddles. "It's fun!"

"And beautiful, too!" said Mother Rabbit. "Look up there!"

"Wow!" said Nathan. "It's great!"

"It's blue and green and yellow and orange and red," said Nora.

"With white clouds, too," said Nellie.

"And it's right near our house, so we won't get lost," said Ned.

"It's a rainbow," explained Mother Rabbit.
"You see them sometimes, right after it has rained."
"Then let's go to the rainbow," said Nicky.
"No, no," said Mother Rabbit. "That's impossible."
"Maybe not," said Nicky. "We could try!"

And that's just what they did.

For Davy Sidjanski

Copyright © 2002 by Valeri Gorbachev

A CHESHIRE STUDIO BOOK
Published in the United States by North-South Books Inc., New York. Published simultaneously in
Great Britain, Canada, Australia, and New Zealand in 2002 by Nord-Süd Verlag AG, Gossau Zürich, Switzerland.
Library of Congress Cataloging-in-Publication Data is available. A CIP catalogue record for this book is available from The British Library.
ISBN 0-7358-1644-1 (trade edition)
1 3 5 7 9 HC 10 8 6 4 2
ISBN 0-7358-1645-X (library edition)
1 3 5 7 9 LE 10 8 6 4 2
Printed in Belgium